Duck and Rooster Go to School

Written by Jill Eggleton
Illustrated by Kelvin Hawley

Rigby

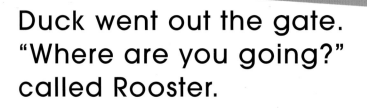

Duck went out the gate.
"Where are you going?"
called Rooster.

"I'm going to school,"
said Duck.

"What for?" said Rooster.

"I haven't been to school,"
said Duck.

Rooster got off the fence.
"I'm coming with you,"
he said.

So Duck and Rooster went
down the road.

When they got to school, the kids were inside.

Duck went **tap-tap** on the window with her bill.

The kids looked out
the window.
"A duck and a rooster
are at school!" they shouted.

When the teacher
opened the window,
Duck and Rooster flew
into the classroom.
They sat on
the teacher's table.

The kids laughed and
the teacher did, too.
"I will tell Mr. Tom to take
them out," she said.

The teacher looked at
Duck and Rooster.
"We can't have you
at school," she said.
"There are too many kids!"

The teacher called Mr. Tom
on her phone.
Duck and Rooster sat very still
on the table.

The teacher said to the kids,
"We could have a look
at this duck and rooster.
What can you see?"

All the kids came up to Duck and Rooster.

They looked at

. . . their heads,

. . . their feathers

and their feet.

Mr. Tom opened the door.

Duck went **_whooooosh_** under his legs!
Rooster went **_whooooosh_** over his head!

Duck and Rooster went
down the road fast.
"We have been to school,"
said Duck.

"I won't be going back,"
said Rooster.
"I'm staying on my fence!"

A Comic Strip

Guide Notes

Title: Duck and Rooster Go to School
Stage: Early (4) – Green

Genre: Fiction
Approach: Guided Reading
Processes: Thinking Critically, Exploring Language, Processing Information
Written and Visual Focus: Comic Strip, Speech Bubbles
Word Count: 240

THINKING CRITICALLY
(sample questions)
- What do you think this story could be about? Look at the title and discuss.
- Look at the cover. What do you think could happen if a duck and rooster went to school?
- Look at pages 2 and 3. How do you know Rooster is nosy?
- Look at page 5. Why do you think Duck went *tap-tap* on the window?
- Look at pages 6 and 7. How do you think the kids feel about a duck and rooster being at their school?
- Look at pages 8 and 9. Why else do you think they couldn't have Duck and Rooster at school?
- Look at page 11. Why do you think the teacher said, "We could have a look at this duck and rooster"?
- Look at page 13. Why do you think Duck and Rooster went *whooooosh* out the door?
- Look at page 14. Why do you think Rooster does not want to go back to school?

EXPLORING LANGUAGE

Terminology
Title, cover, illustrations, author, illustrator

Vocabulary
Interest words: fence, bill, tap, teacher, table, phone, feathers
High-frequency words: called, won't, still, tell, could
Positional words: on, inside, down, into, out, off, up, under, over
Compound word: inside

Print Conventions
Capital letter for sentence beginnings and names (**M**r. **T**om, **D**uck, **R**ooster), periods, commas, exclamation marks, quotation marks, question marks, ellipsis, possessive apostrophe